Clifford The BIG RED DOG®

WATCH ON prime video · PBS KIDS

Clifford's Snow Day

Clifford created by
Norman Bridwell

Scholastic Inc.

Written by
Reika Chan

Copyright © 2021 by Scholastic Entertainment Inc.
CLIFFORD, CLIFFORD THE BIG RED DOG, and associated logos are trademarks and/or registered trademarks of The Norman Bridwell Trust.

PBS KIDS and PBS KIDS logo are trademarks of Public Broadcasting Service. Used with permission.

ISBN 978-1-338-76475-8

10 9 8 7 6 5 4 3 2 1   21 22 23 24 25

Printed in Jefferson City, MO, U.S.A. 40 • First edition 2021

Book design by Veronica Mang & Salena Mahina

Scholastic Inc., 557 Broadway, New York, NY 10012
Scholastic UK Ltd., Euston House, 24 Eversholt Street, London NW1 1DB
Scholastic LTD, Unit 89E, Lagan Road, Dublin Industrial Estate, Glasnevin, Dublin 11

It was a beautiful winter day on Birdwell Island. Emily Elizabeth and Clifford were playing Rescue Squad together.

"We've got to help Mr. Nibbles down the tree!" Emily Elizabeth said.

"Good thing helping is what we do best!" Clifford replied.

Then Clifford and Emily Elizabeth saw Fire Chief Franklin drive by. His firedog, Tucker, was kicking salt onto the road from the back of the fire truck.

"What are you and Tucker doing, Fire Chief Franklin?" Emily Elizabeth asked.

"A big snowstorm is on its way," he explained. "The salt will help melt the snow on the roads. We might get more snow than we've ever had!"

Emily Elizabeth rushed home to read her Birdwell Island almanac.
"What's an *almond yak*?" Clifford asked.

Emily Elizabeth giggled. "An *almanac* is a book that tells you about the weather in a place."

The almanac said that a heavy snowstorm on Birdwell Island was rare, but possible!

Emily Elizabeth couldn't wait for the snow. But Clifford wasn't so sure. He had never seen snow before. What if it was too cold or too slippery?

Just then, tiny snowflakes started to fall from the sky.

Clifford watched as a snowflake landed on his tongue and melted.

It was a little cold—but it was fun, too! Clifford was starting to feel excited about the snow.

The snow continued to fall.

Before long, Birdwell Island had turned into a winter wonderland!

"Come on, let's go play!" Emily Elizabeth told Clifford.

Clifford and Emily Elizabeth
built a snowman and made
snow angels.

Clifford pulled Emily Elizabeth along the snowy streets on her snowboard.

And Emily Elizabeth sledded down Clifford-sized piles of snow!

"You were right, Emily Elizabeth!" Clifford said.
"Snow is so . . . so . . ."

ACHOO!

Emily Elizabeth touched Clifford's nose. It felt dry and warm.
"I think you might be coming down with a little cold," she said.

Just then, they noticed Fire Chief Franklin trying to push his truck out of a snow drift.

Clifford ran over and helped get the truck unstuck. "Thanks, Clifford!" Fire Chief Franklin said.

Fire Chief Franklin wasn't the only person having trouble because of the snow.

Slippery roads made it dangerous to drive. Piles of snow blocked front doors. And some of the forest animals were very cold.

Clifford had an idea. "Maybe we could play Rescue Squad for real! We could help anyone in trouble—achoo!"

Emily Elizabeth was worried about Clifford's cold. But Clifford thought helping their friends would make him feel better.

"Then let's do it!" Emily Elizabeth said.

The Birdwell Snow Rescue Squad jumped into action.

Clifford and Emily Elizabeth delivered firewood to Mrs. Clayton.

And Clifford swept away the snow blocking Jack's front door with a giant sneeze.

Clifford's big paws came in handy for clearing the roads.

He gave Mr. Basu's mail truck a boost up a slippery hill.

And when the Birdwell Snow Rescue Squad visited the forest, the critters snuggled up into Clifford's warm fur.

But the whole time they were helping their friends, Clifford couldn't stop sneezing.

Ah, ah, ACHOOOOOO!

"Your little cold doesn't seem so little anymore," Emily Elizabeth said.

It was time for Clifford to go home and rest.

Back in his doghouse, Clifford was sad he couldn't help more people. "I feel like I let everybody down," he told Emily Elizabeth.

Then they heard visitors at the front of the house.

"You two were so kind to help everyone today," Fire Chief Franklin said to Emily Elizabeth and Clifford. "So we decided to return the favor!"

Fire Chief Franklin offered the fire truck's hose to Clifford to use as a big straw. "It is important to stay hydrated!" he said.

Mrs. Clayton brought a bedtime book to help Clifford relax.

Jack made a big batch of veggie soup.

And Mr. Basu brought mail bags to hang on Clifford's ears like giant earmuffs.

The animals from the forest even stopped by to keep Clifford company!
Clifford hadn't let his neighbors down. He had lifted them up!

Clifford smiled, and snowflakes began to fall from the sky again.

"Let it snow!" Emily Elizabeth cheered.

Even in chilly weather, the people on Birdwell Island stayed warm by sticking together!

USA • PO# 5052693 • 07/21